IKE'S INCREDIBLE INK

Brianne Farley

CANDLEWICK PRESS

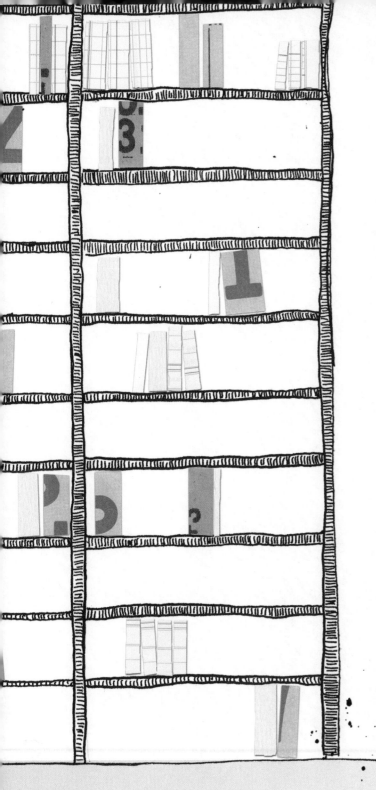

Ike wanted to write a story.

An incredible story.

He had read many incredible stories,

and he felt sure he could write one of his own.

He was ready to start . . .

but what should he write about?

Maybe he needed to find
his favorite pen.

And have a long chat with his best friend.

And a bit of cleaning was
also in order.

But even then, something was wrong.
Something was missing.

"Hmm," said Ike.
"Maybe I need . . ."

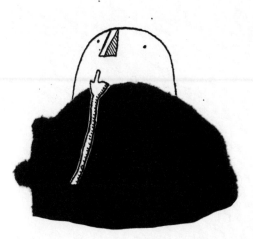

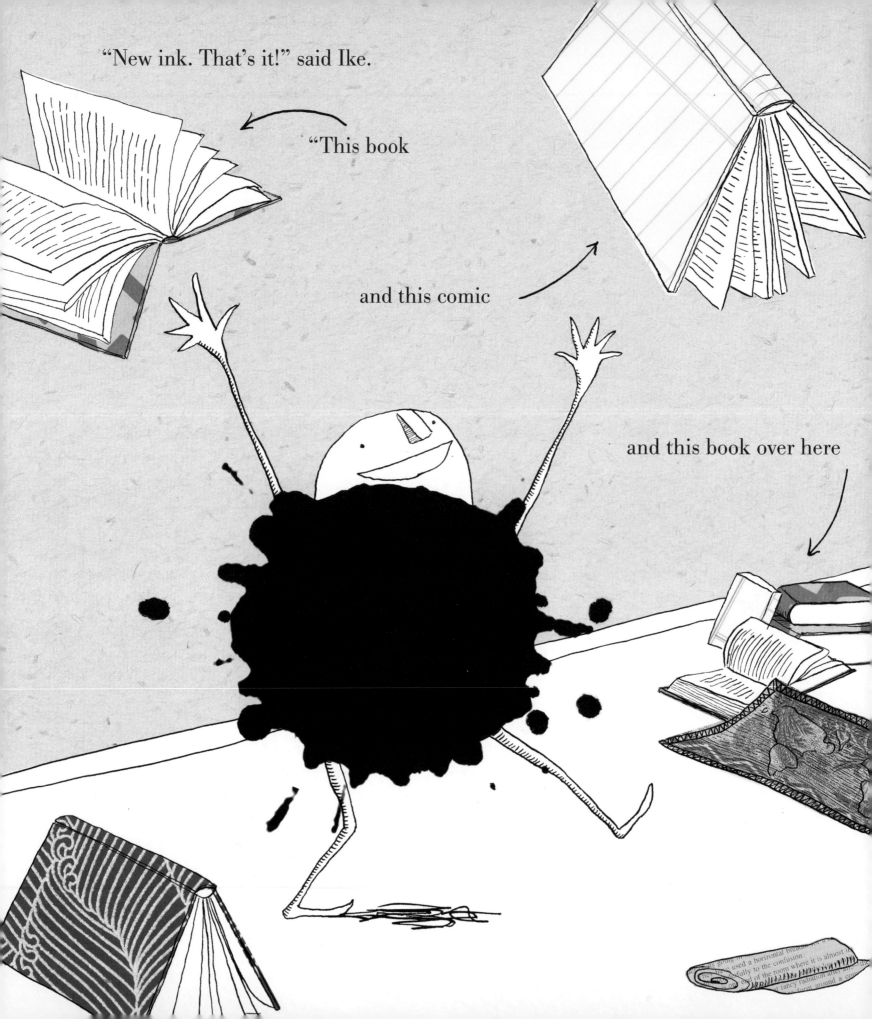

and this map

are all printed with ink. Their *very own* ink.

I need my own ink!"

"First," Ike said, "I need the right ingredients."

He looked around the room.

Shadows, he thought, *are like ink.*

They are shady and shifty and mysterious.

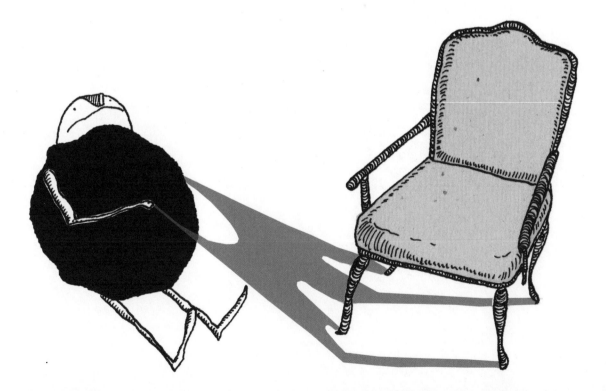

He shook out a shadow and put it in a big bag.

Next, Ike looked outside.
Booga-bird feathers, he thought, *are*
floaty and soft like ink.

So he gave the booga-birds their favorite
treat, took a few feathers, and stuffed
them into his big bag.

Ike looked at the sky. *The dark side of the moon,*
he thought, *is black like ink. It's velvety and pretty*
and round like a drop of ink.

So he decided to go there.

He would, of course, need a rocket ship.

So he doodled and measured and lugged and planned.

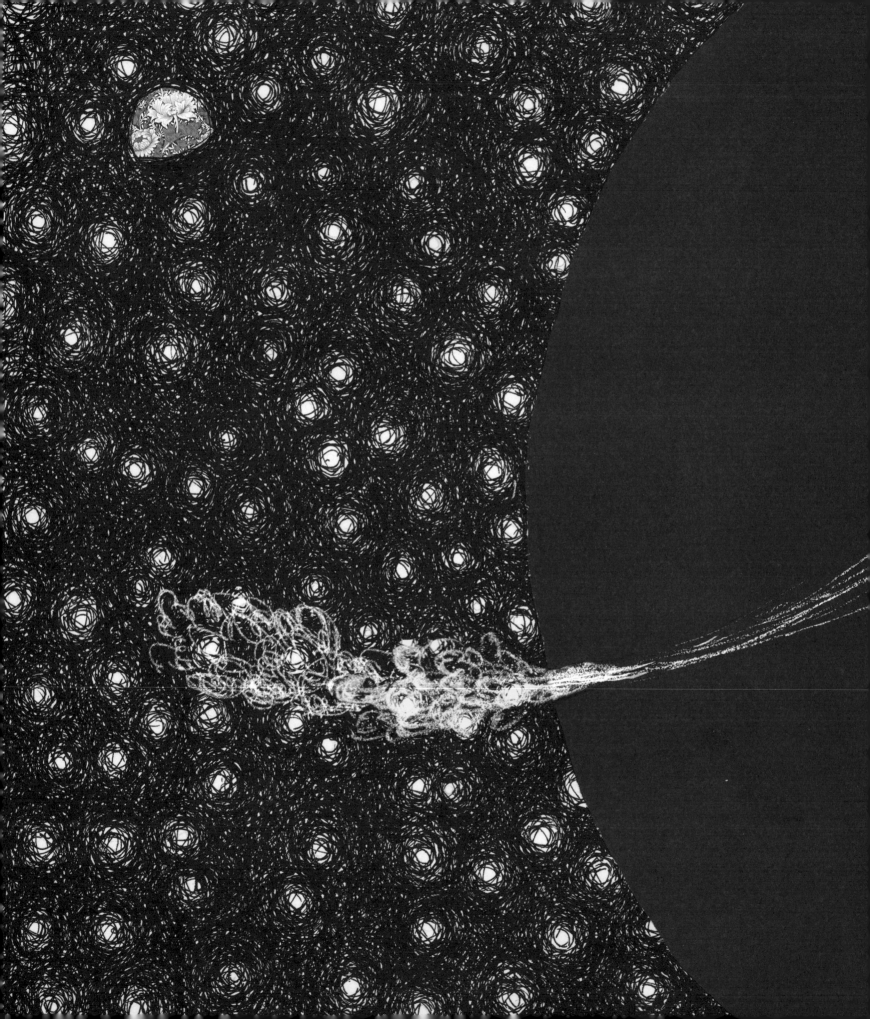

It's hard to say what Ike found on the dark side of the moon, because he didn't bring a flashlight.

But whatever he found went in that big bag.

"Finally," he said. "I have everything I need."

Ike set to work.

He mashed,
he bludgeoned,
he crushed,
and he steamed.

And he was definitely messy.

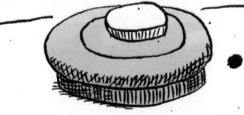

Ike bottled up his ink. It looked pretty good.

He sat back down at his desk . . .

HOW TO
FOLD A
MAP

and he started to write an incredible story.

For Mom and Dad (stargazers)
and for Allan (rocket builder)

First edition 2013

Library of Congress Catalog Card Number 2012947261
ISBN 978-0-7636-6296-7

13 14 15 16 17 18 TLF 10 9 8 7 6 5 4 3 2 1

Printed in Dongguan, Guangdong, China

This book was typeset in Bodoni Antiqua.
The illustrations were done in ink and digital collage.

Candlewick Press
99 Dover Street
Somerville, Massachusetts 02144

visit us at www.candlewick.com